Monday's Child

Michael Bragg

for Cyan Alice Saskia

LONDON
VICTOR GOLLANCZ LTD
1988

Monday's child is fair of face

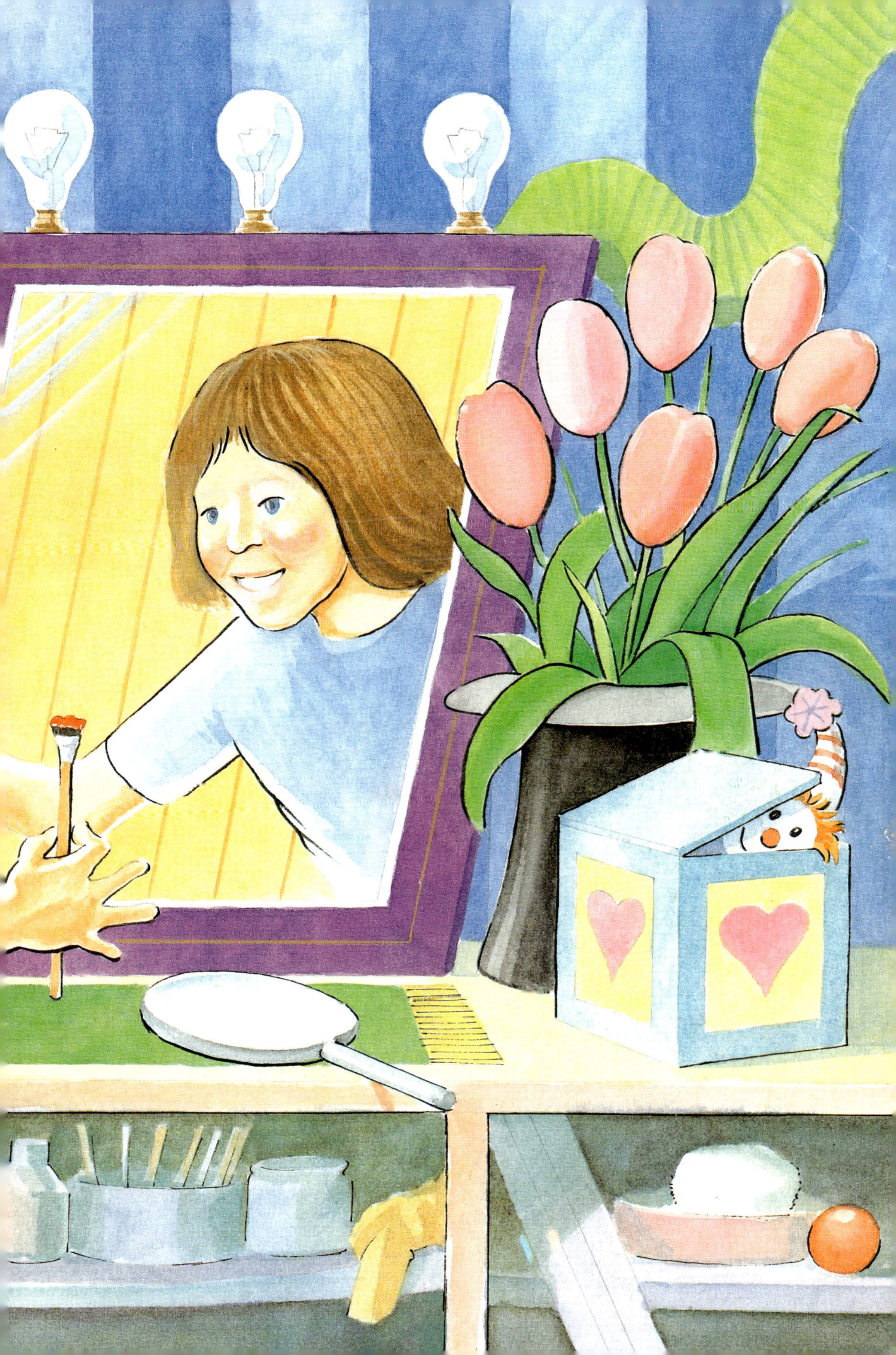

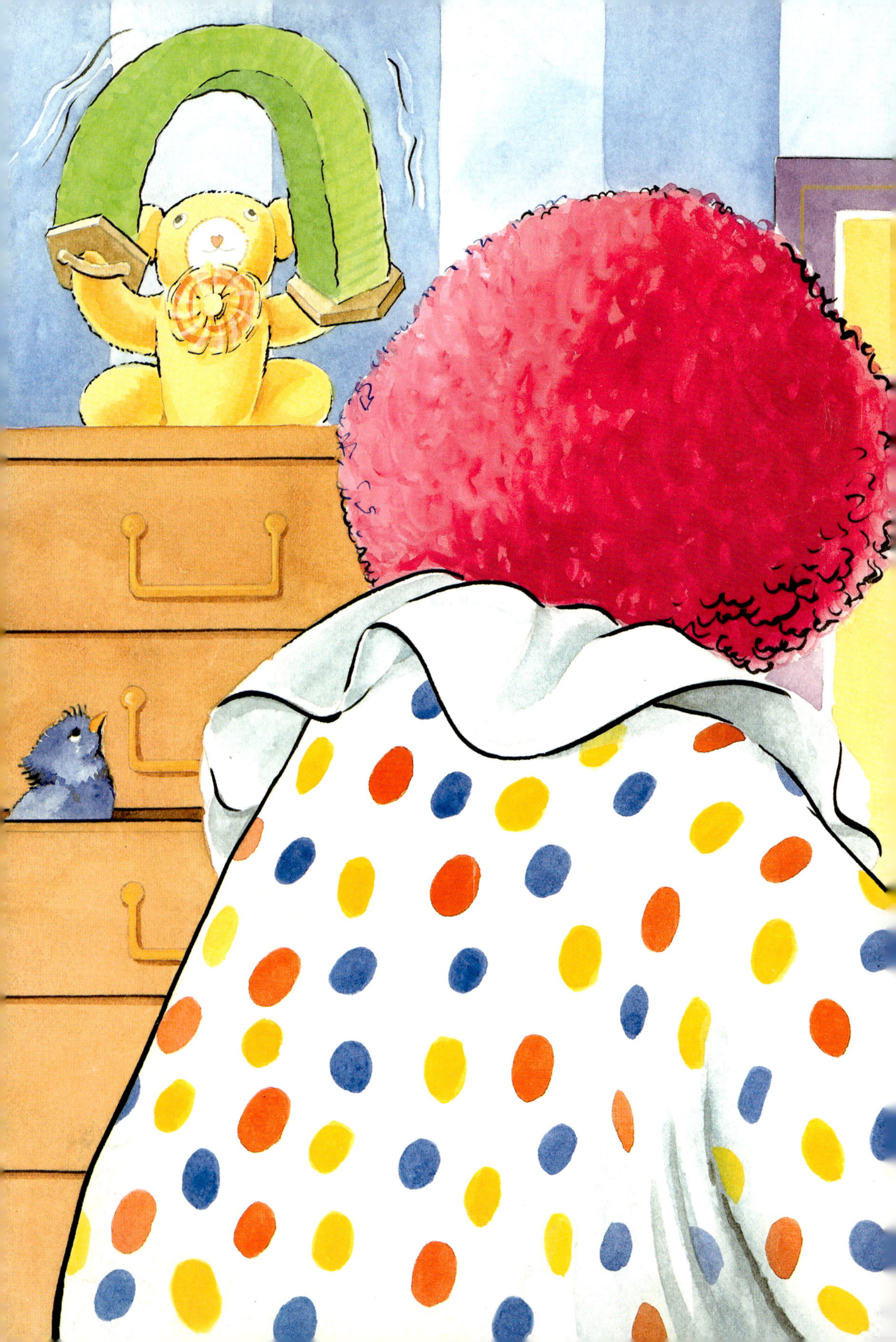

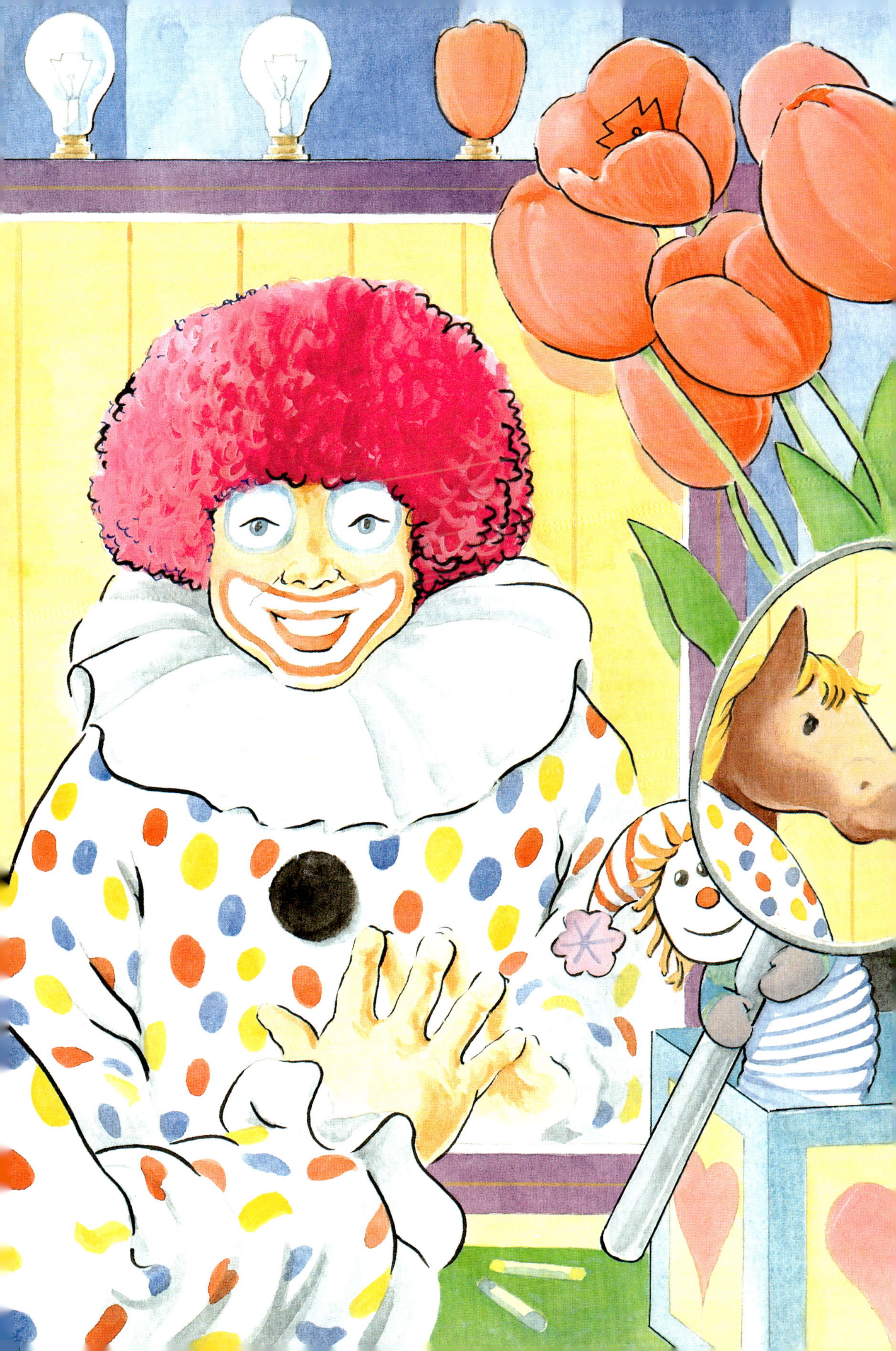

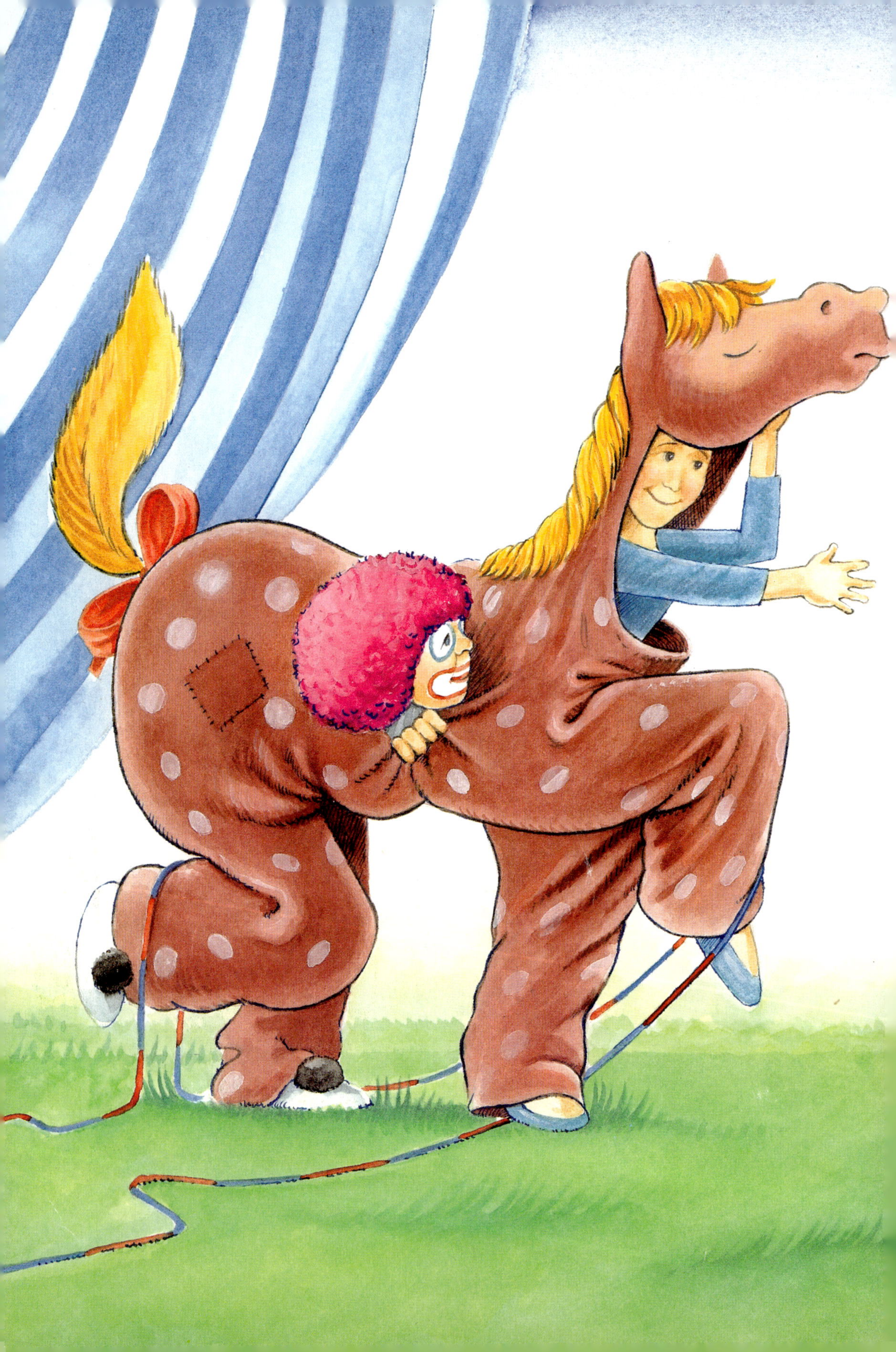

Tuesday's child is full of grace

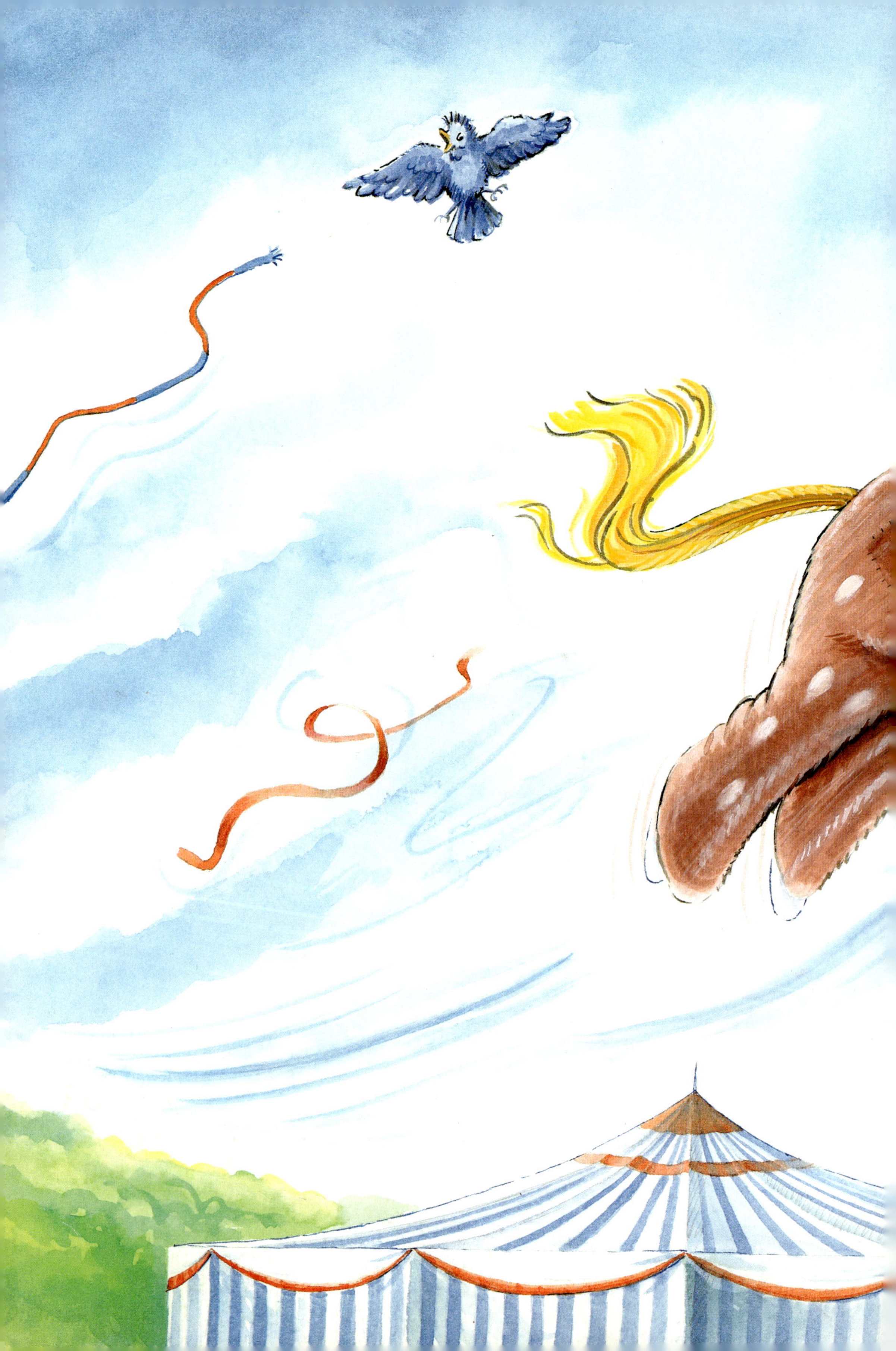

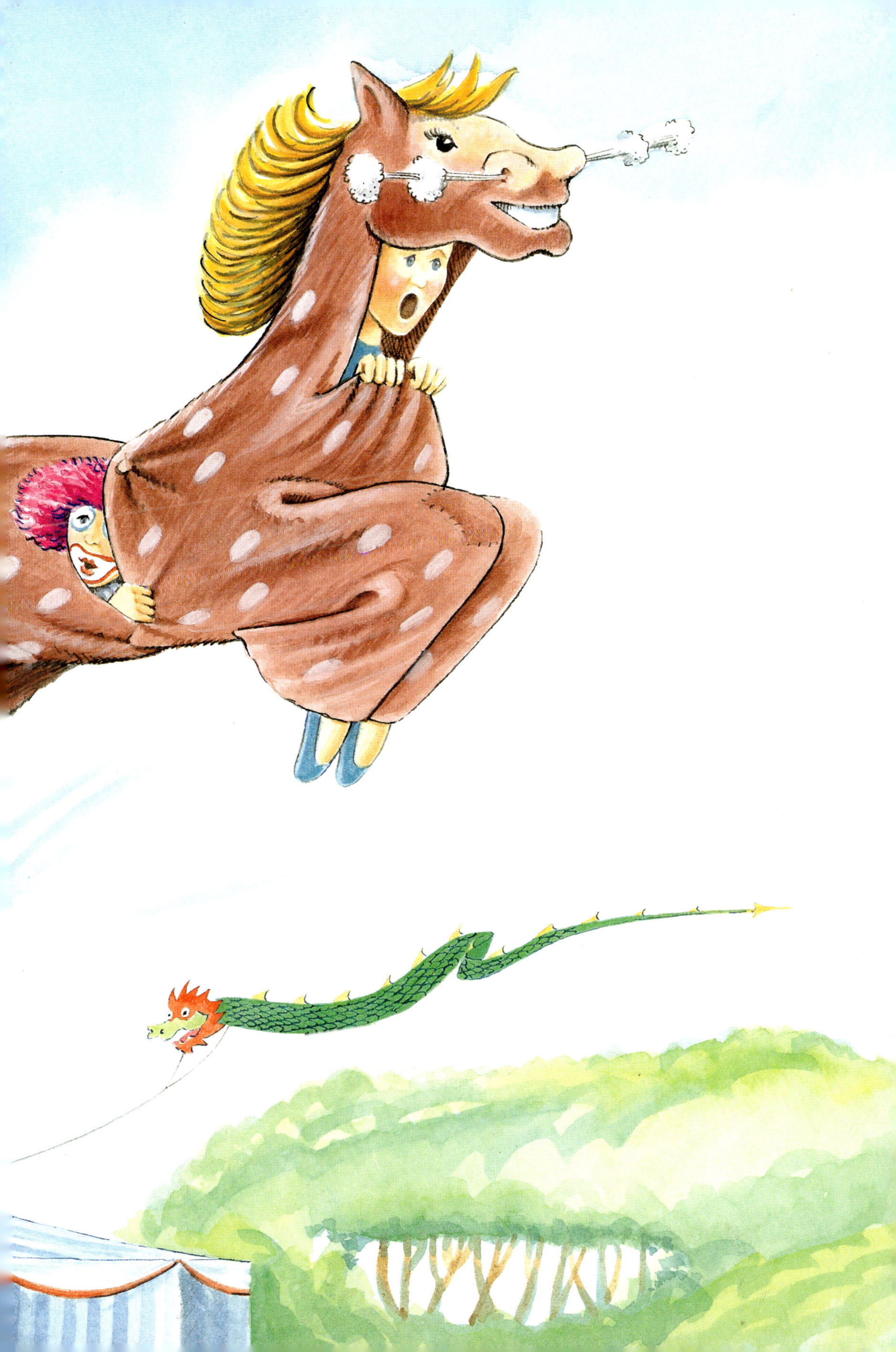

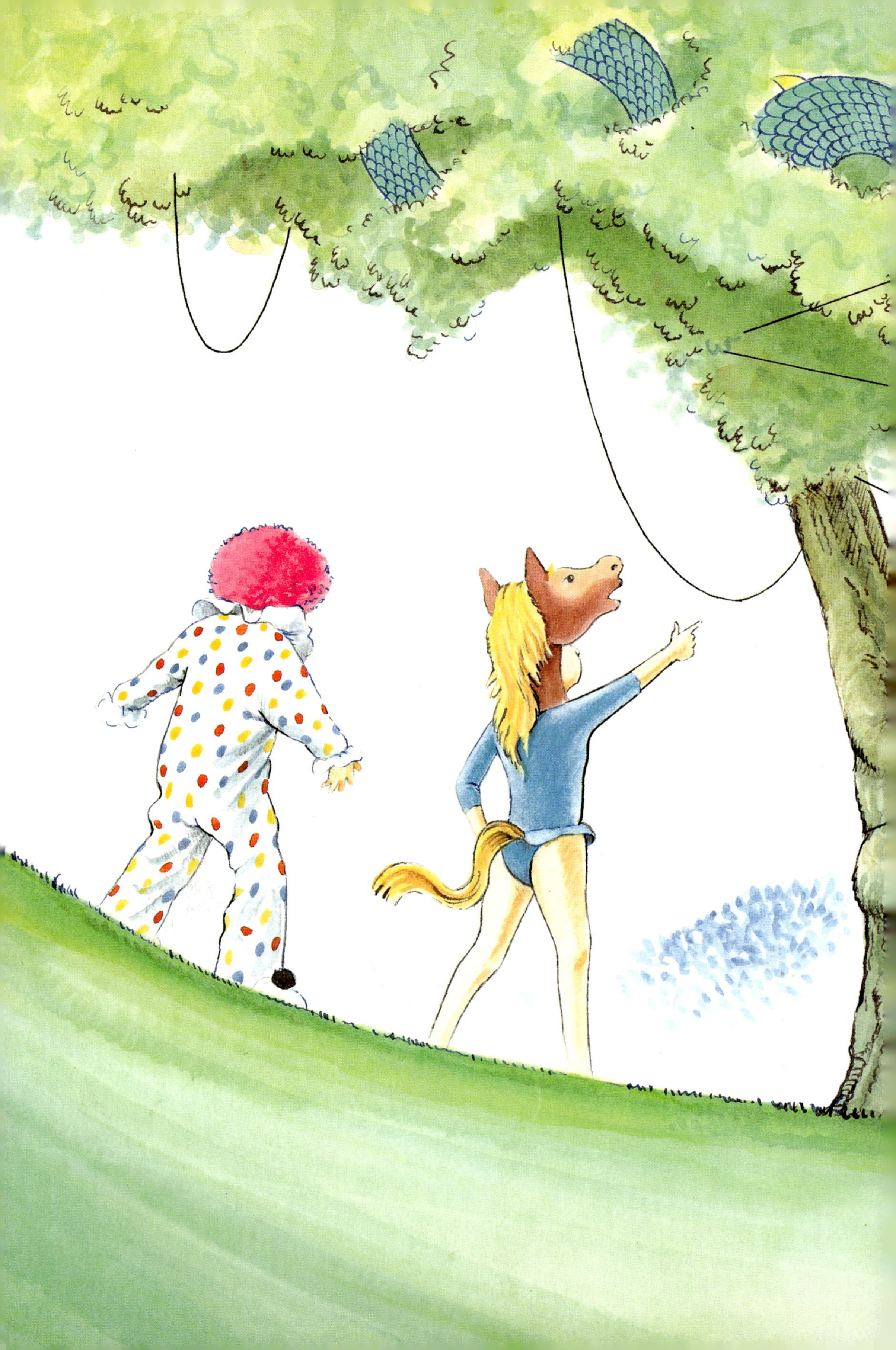

Wednesday's child is full of woe

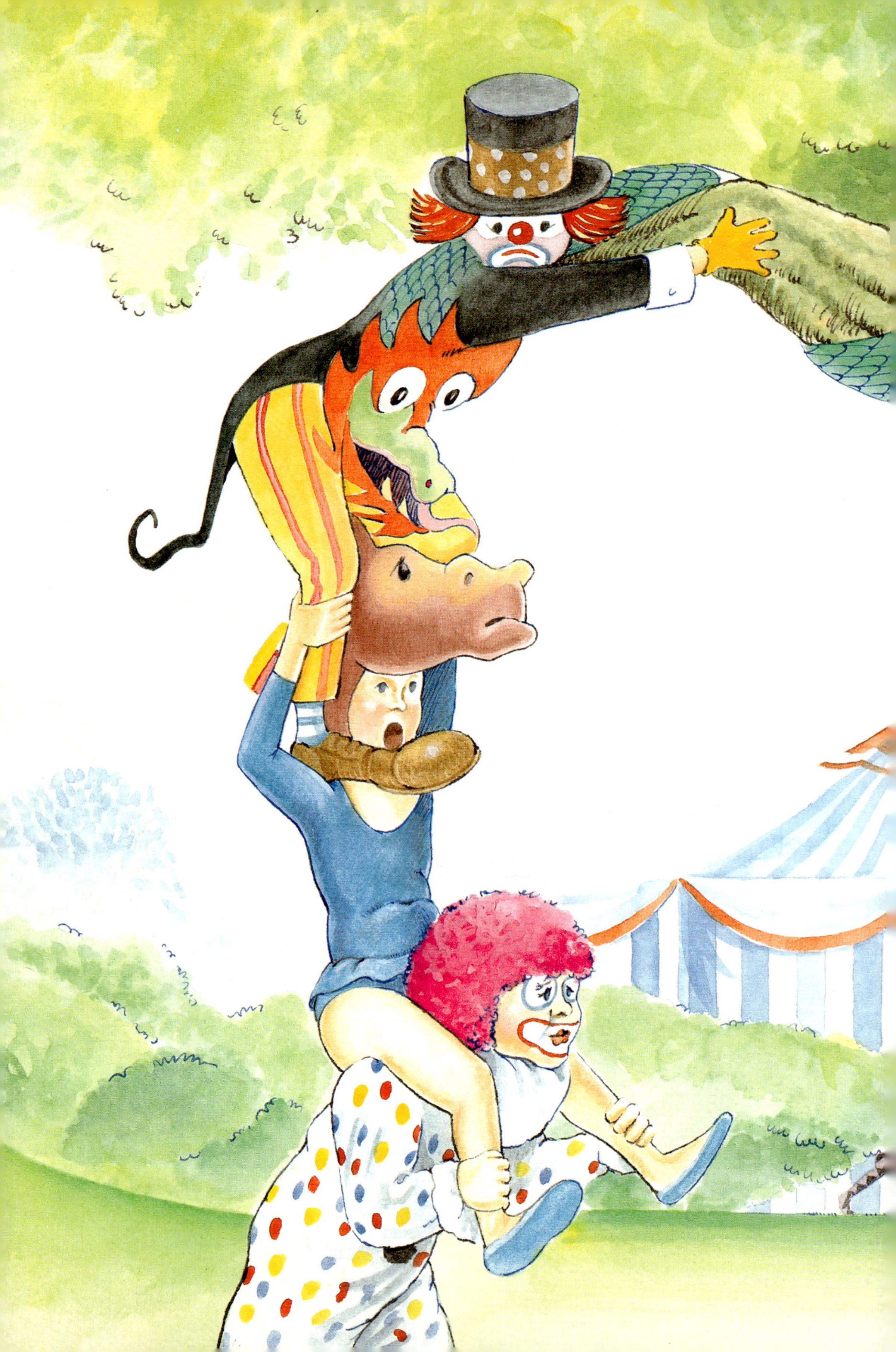

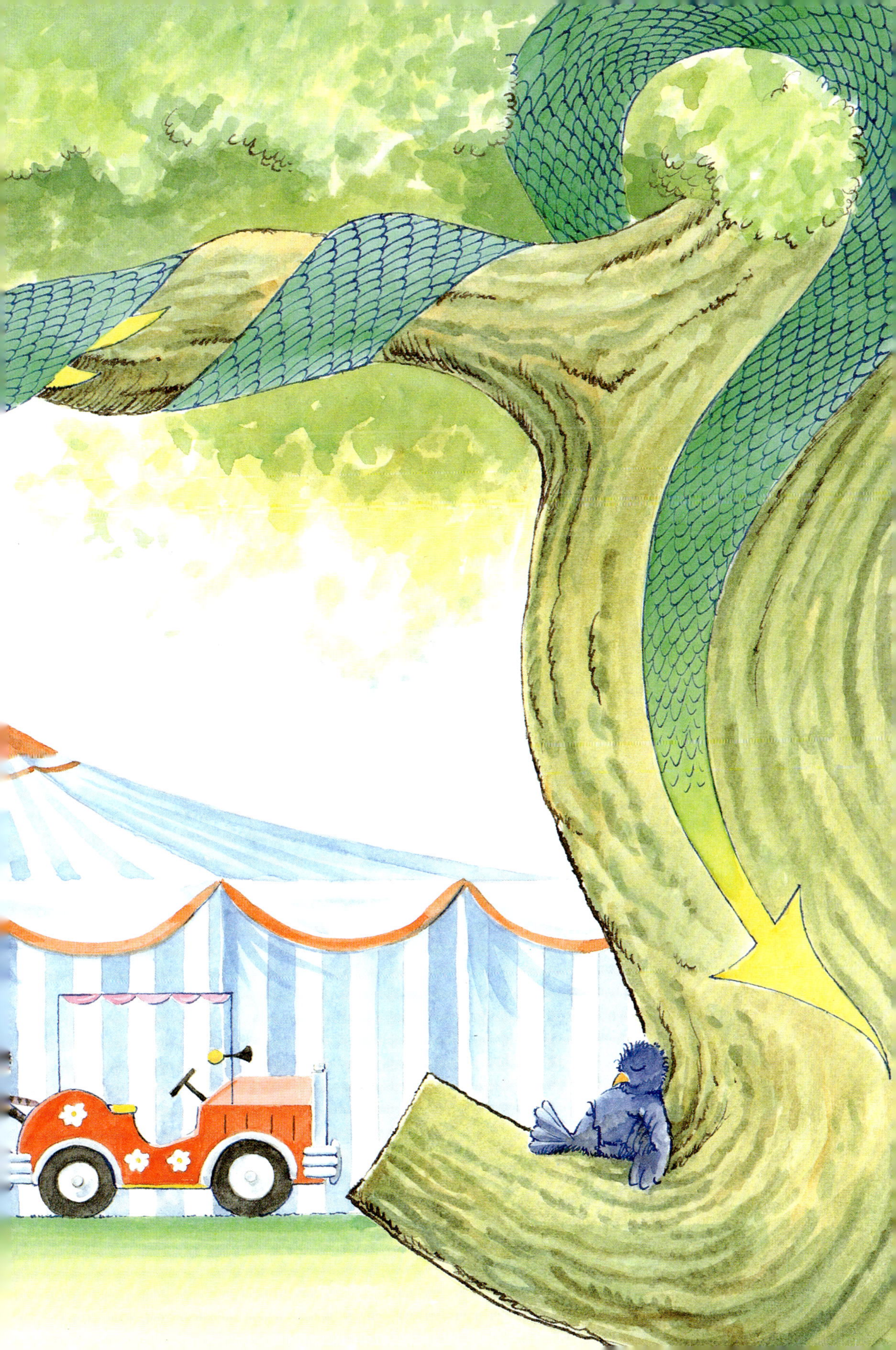

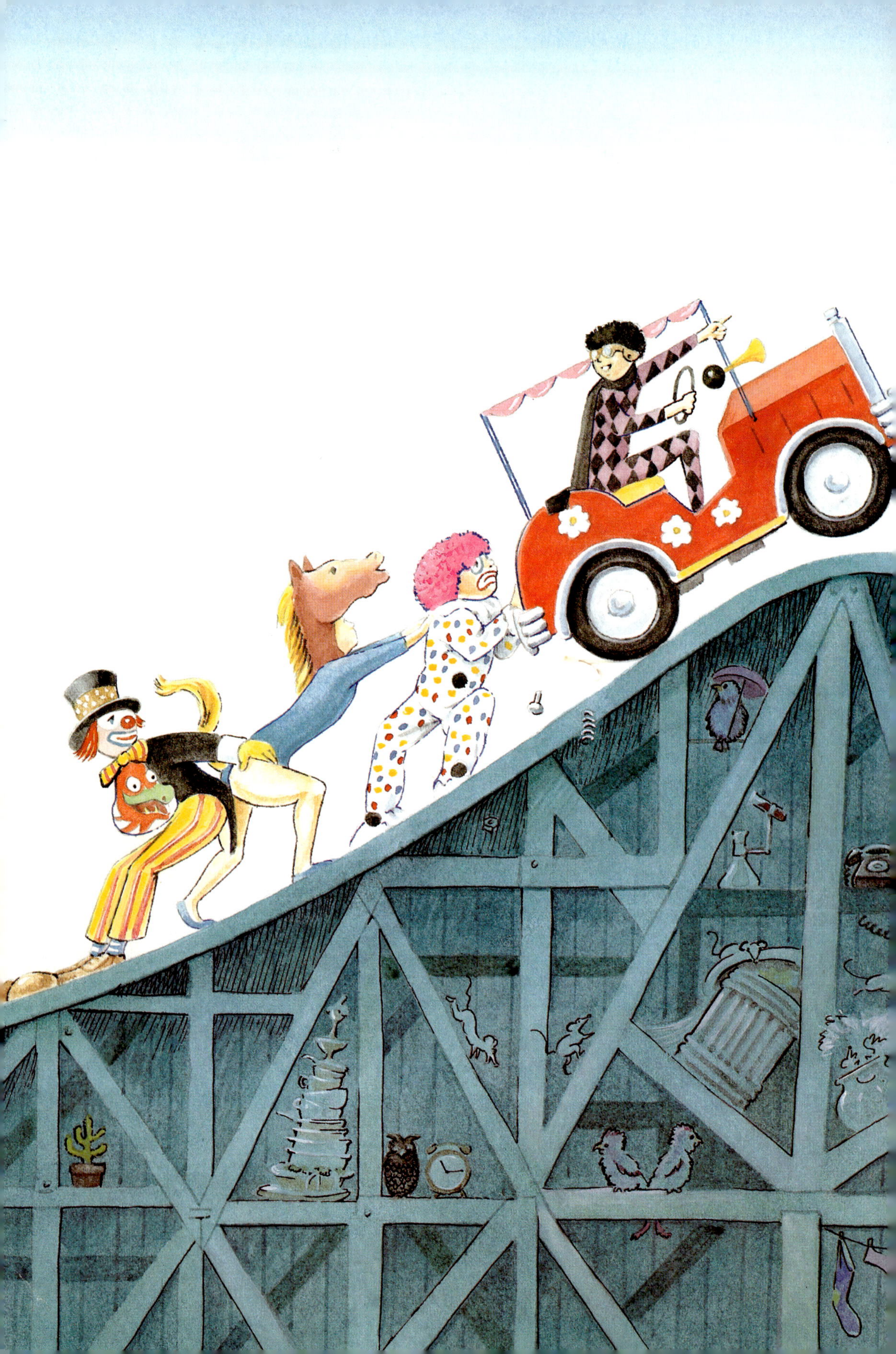

Thursday's child has far to go

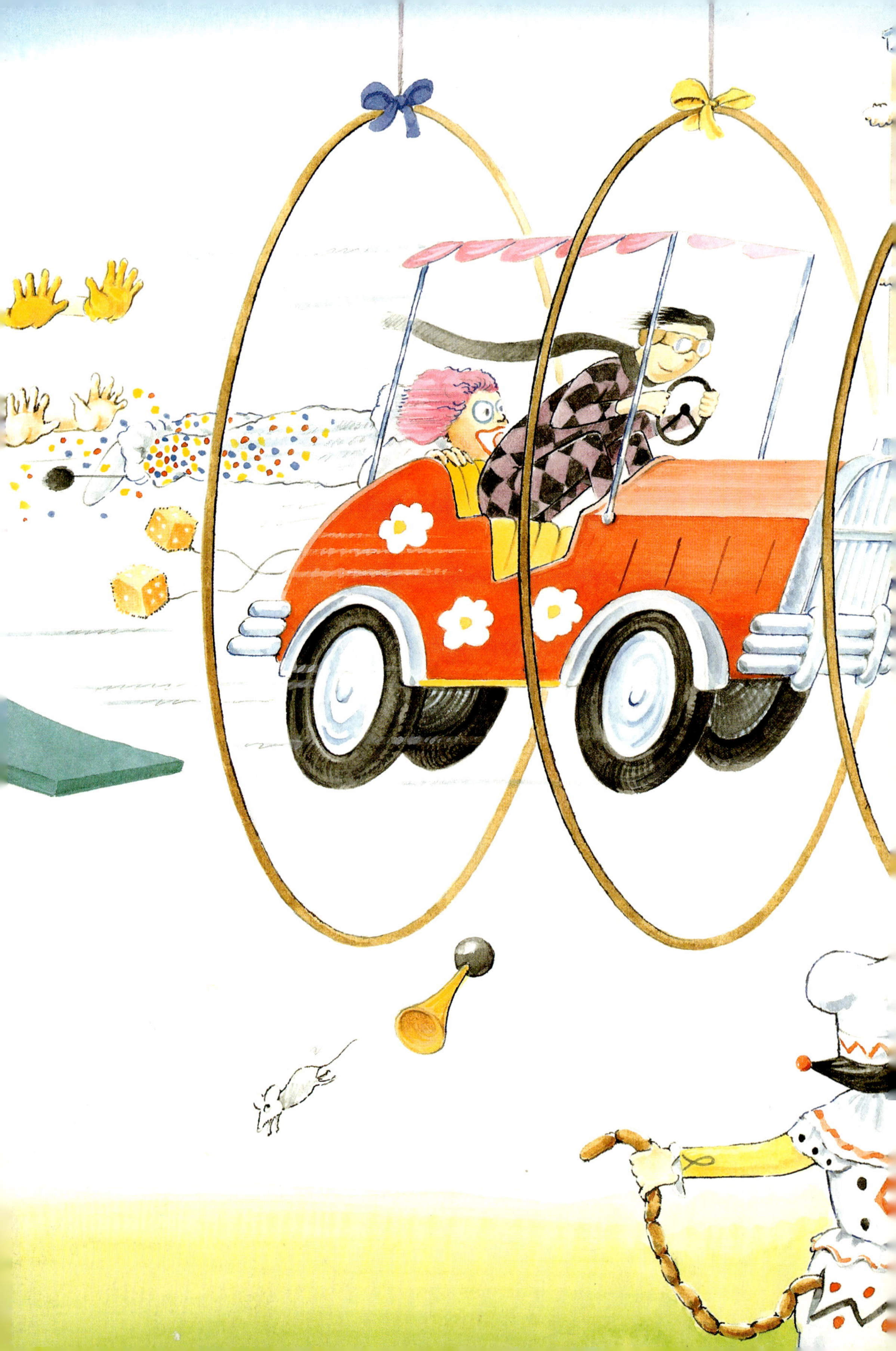

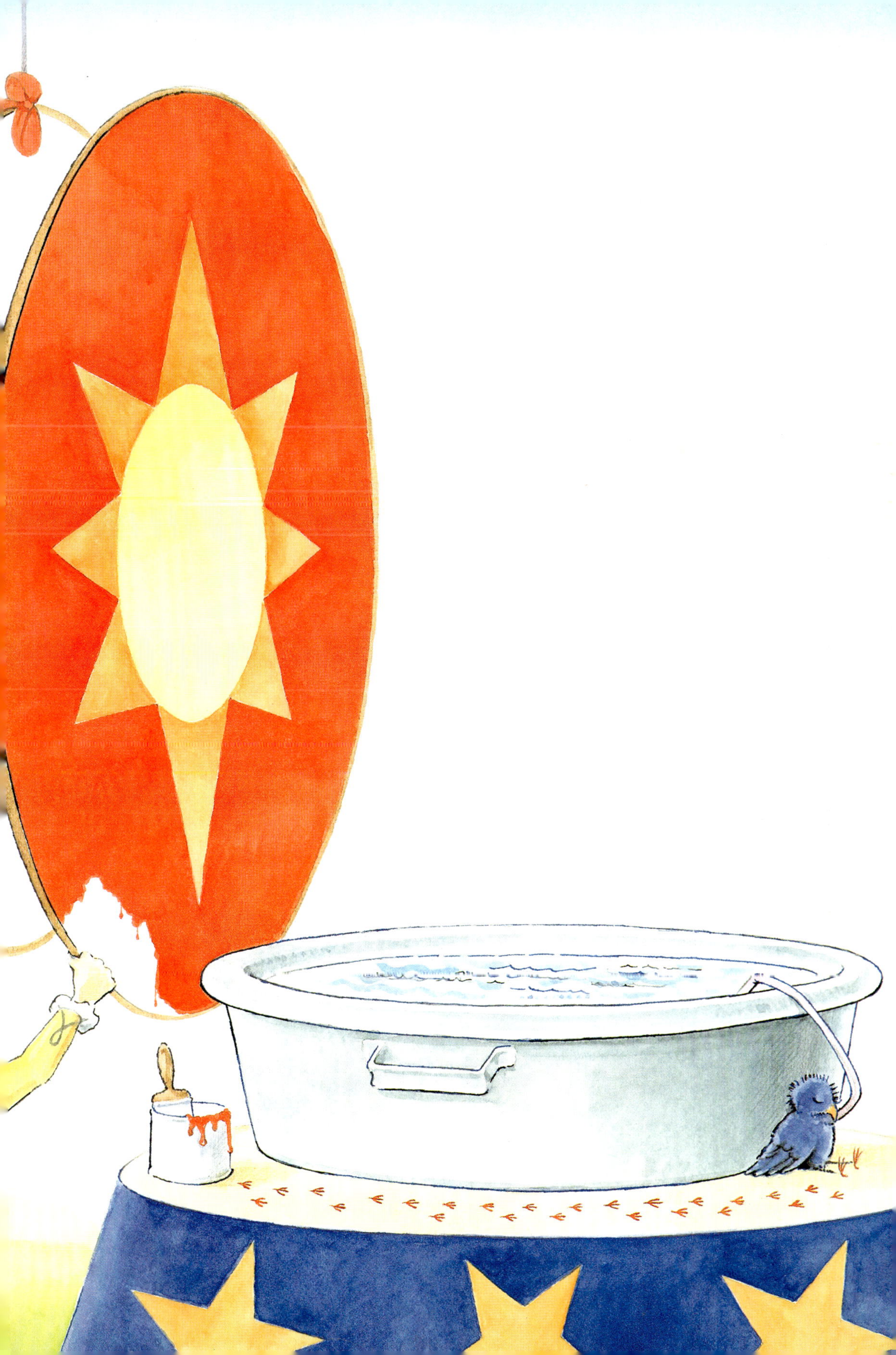

Friday's child is loving and giving

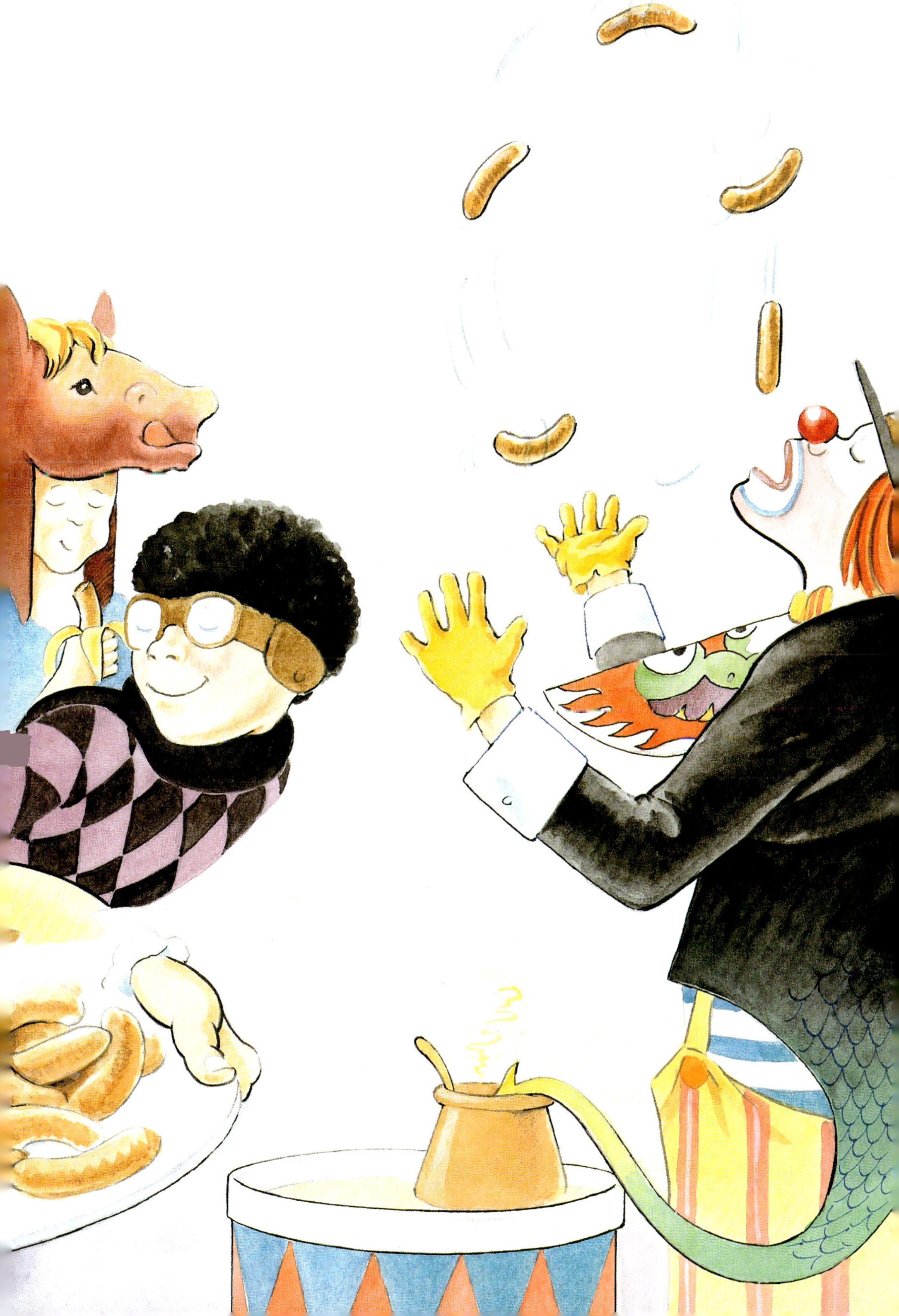

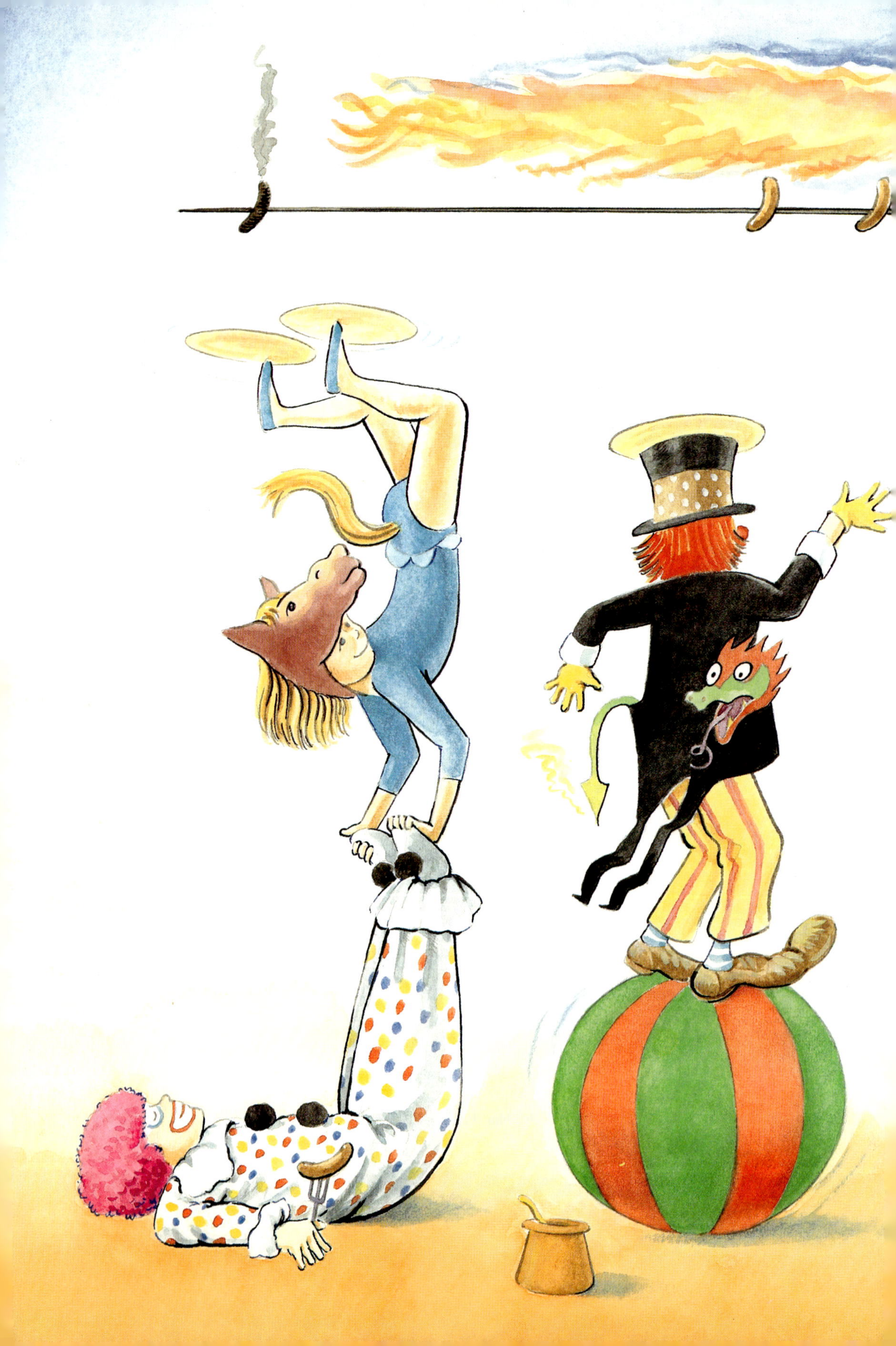

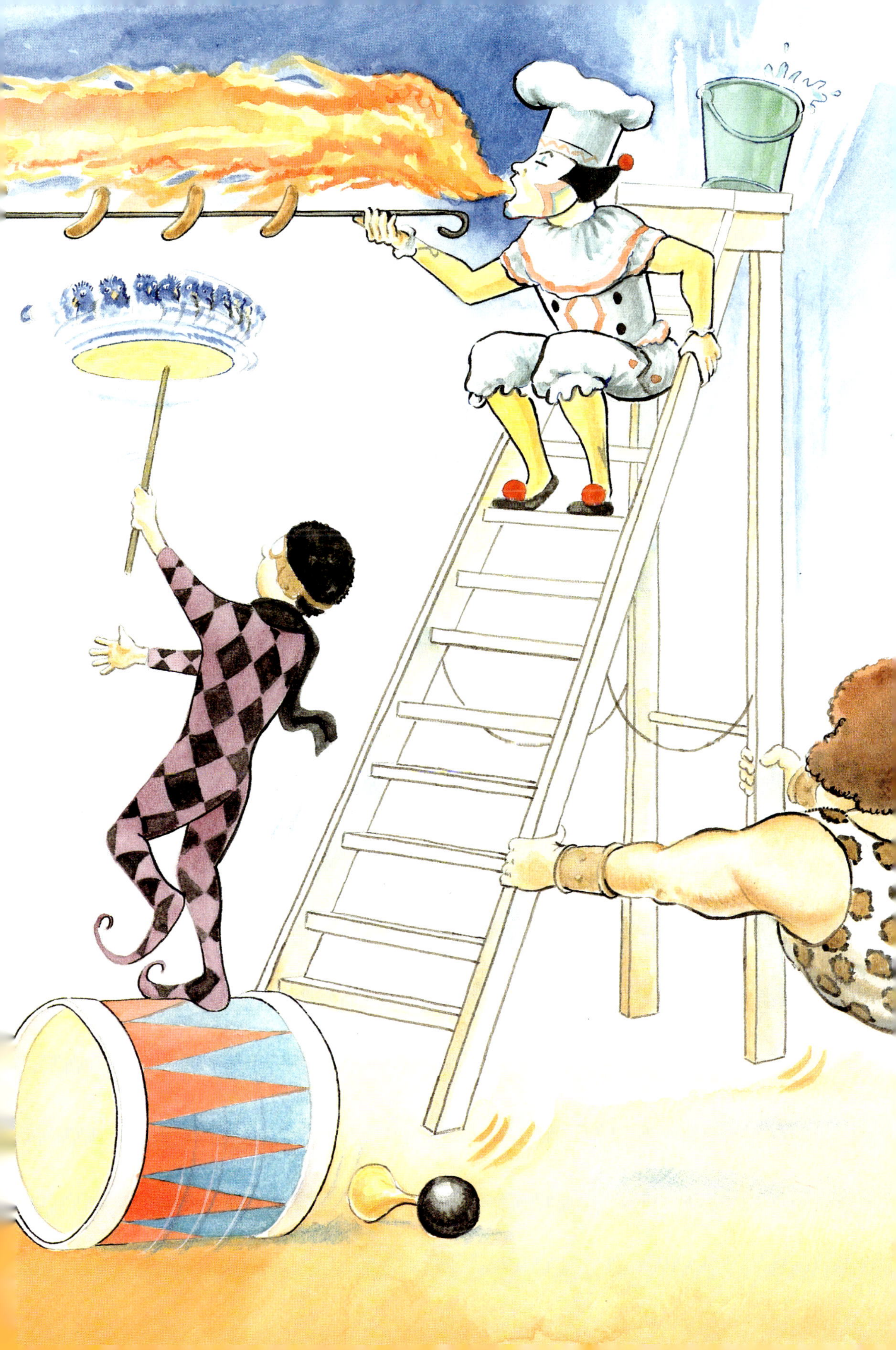

Saturday's child works hard for a living

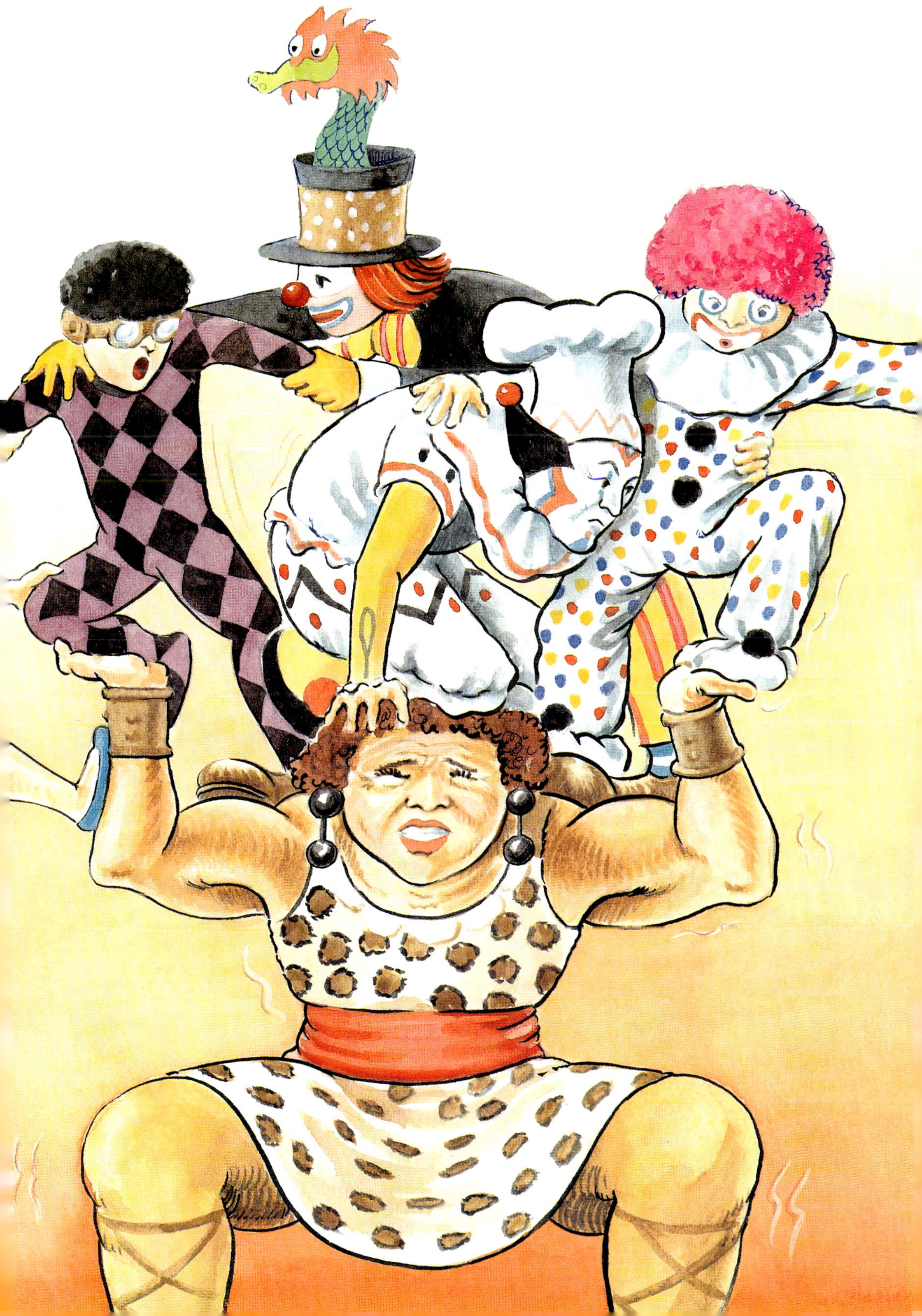

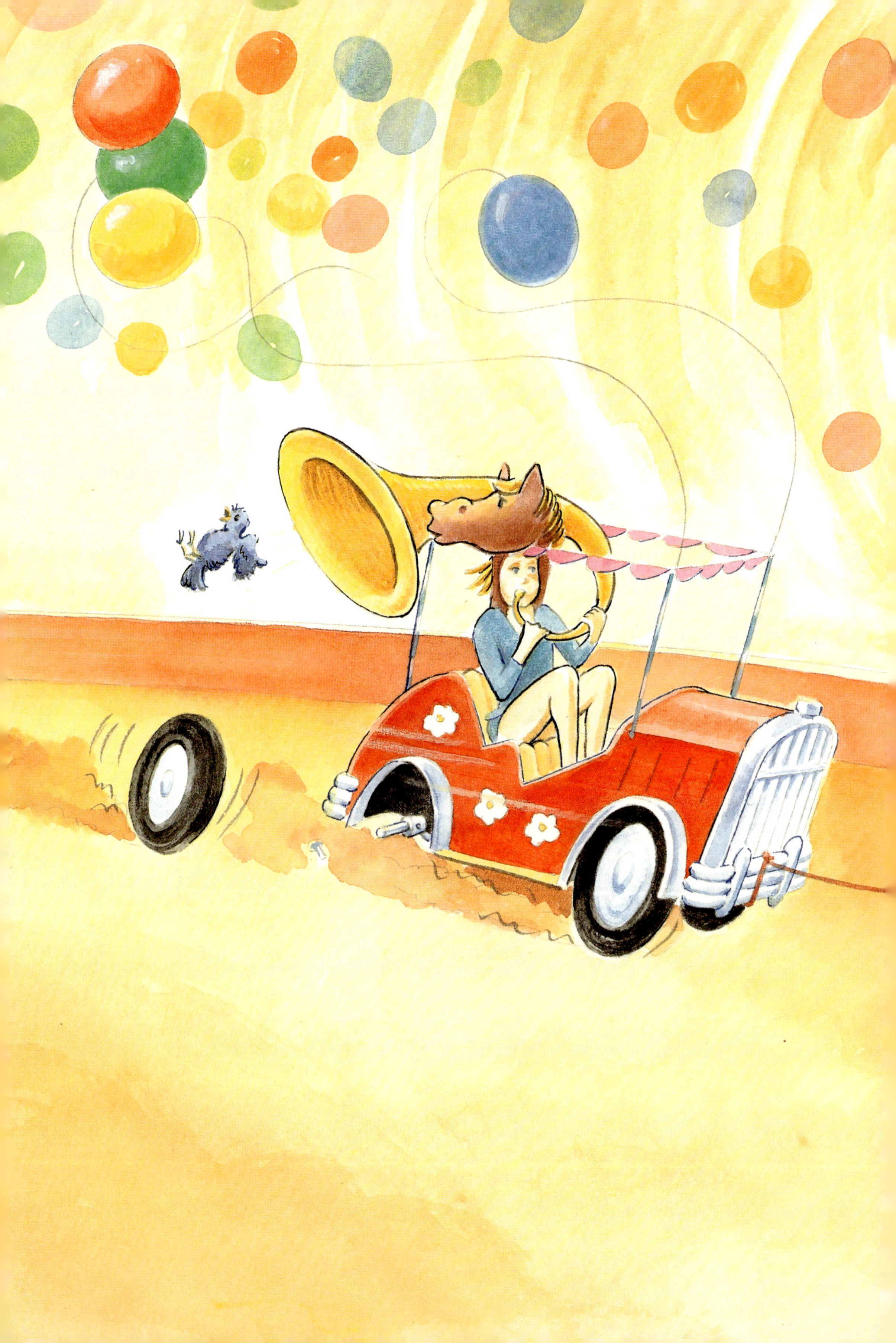

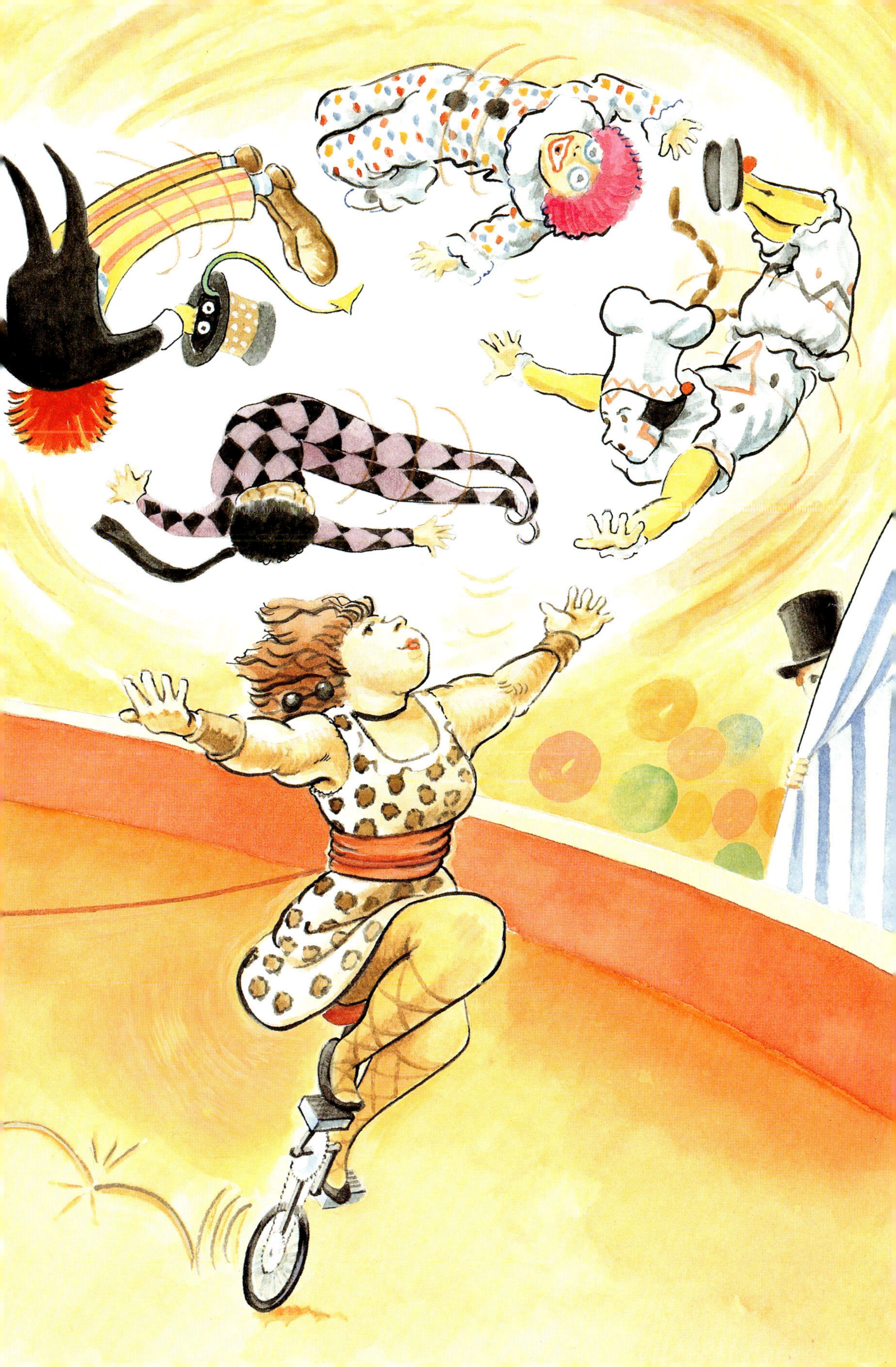

And the child that is born on a Sunday

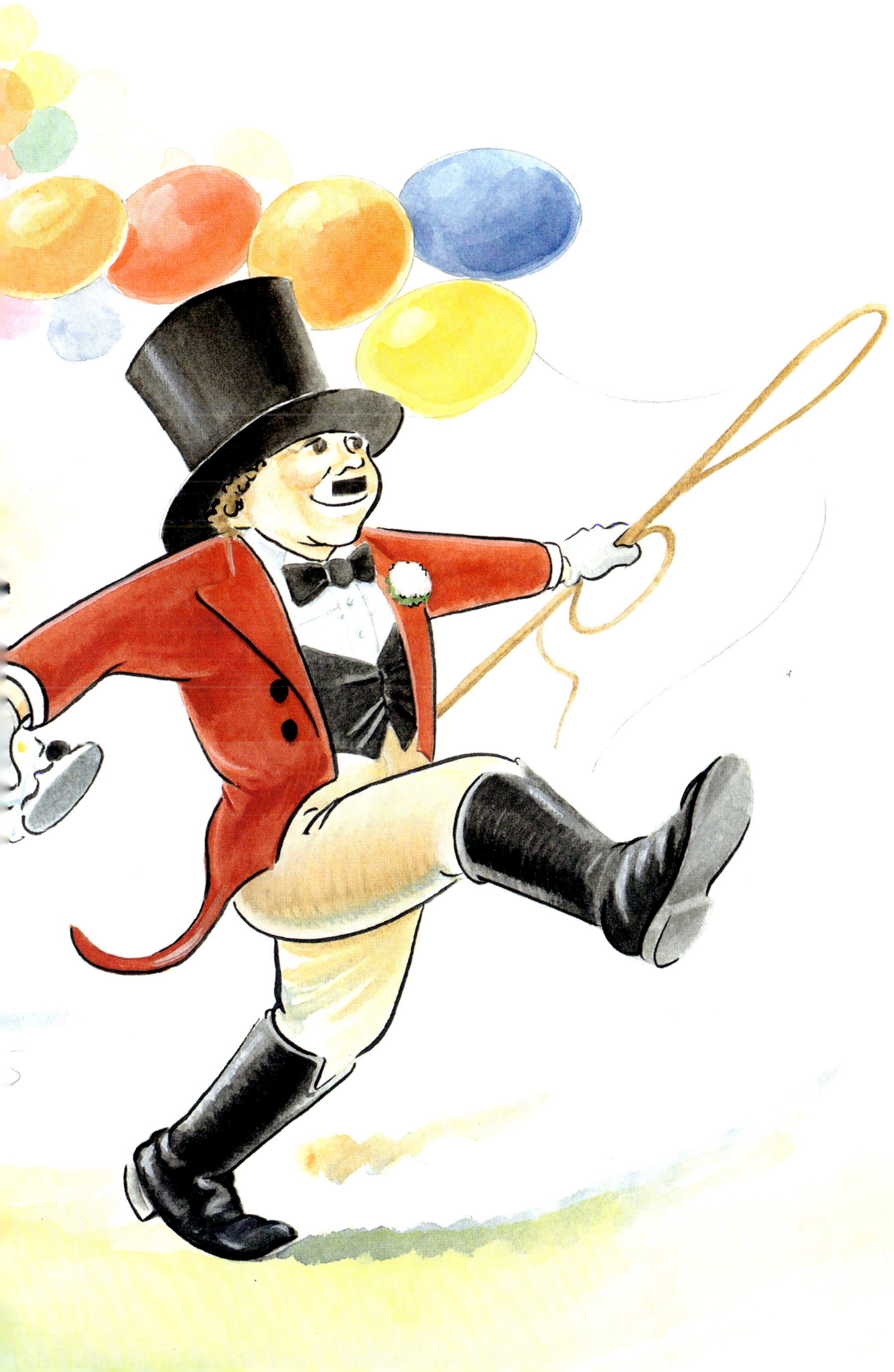

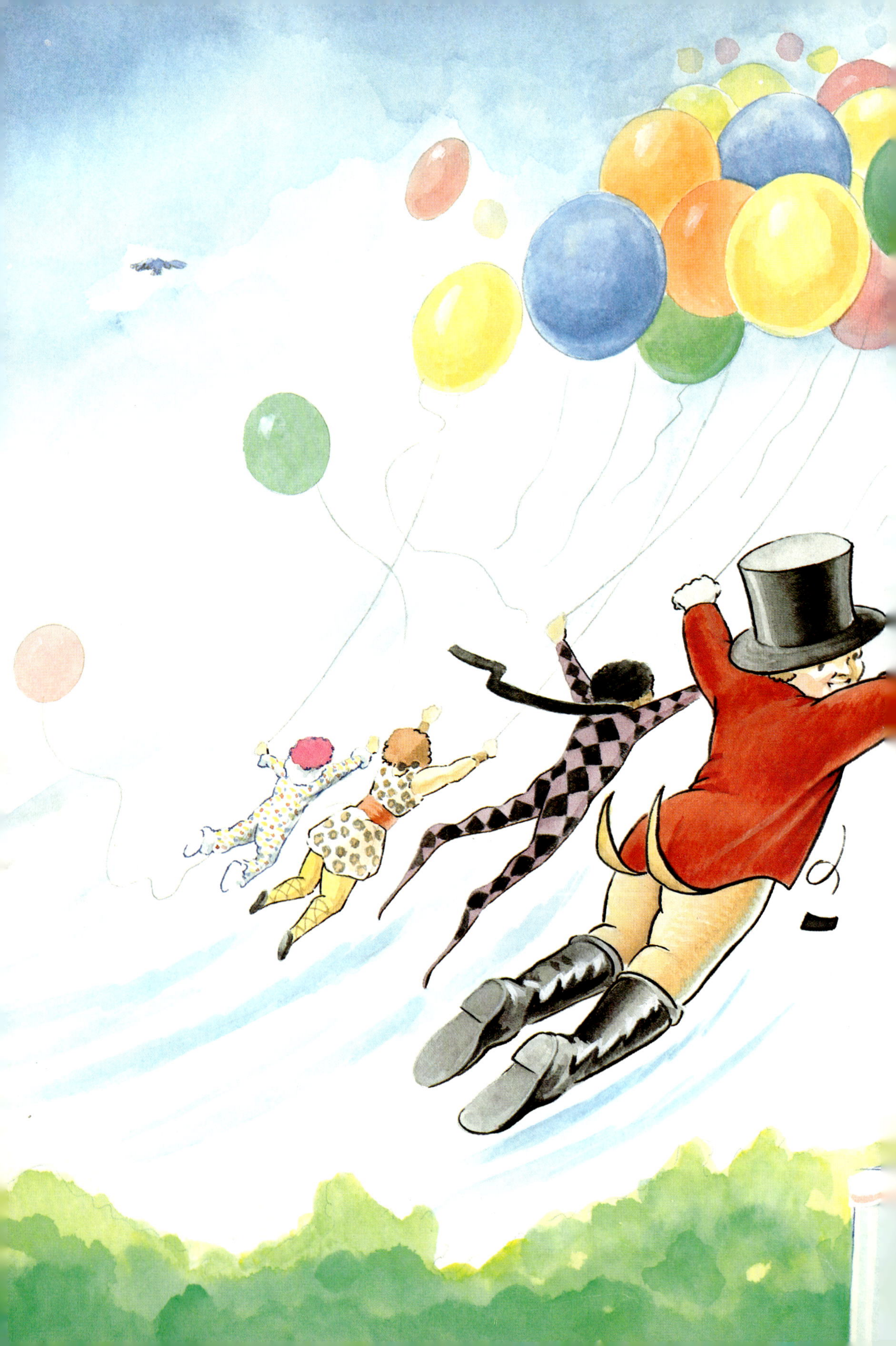

Is bonny and blithe

and good and gay.

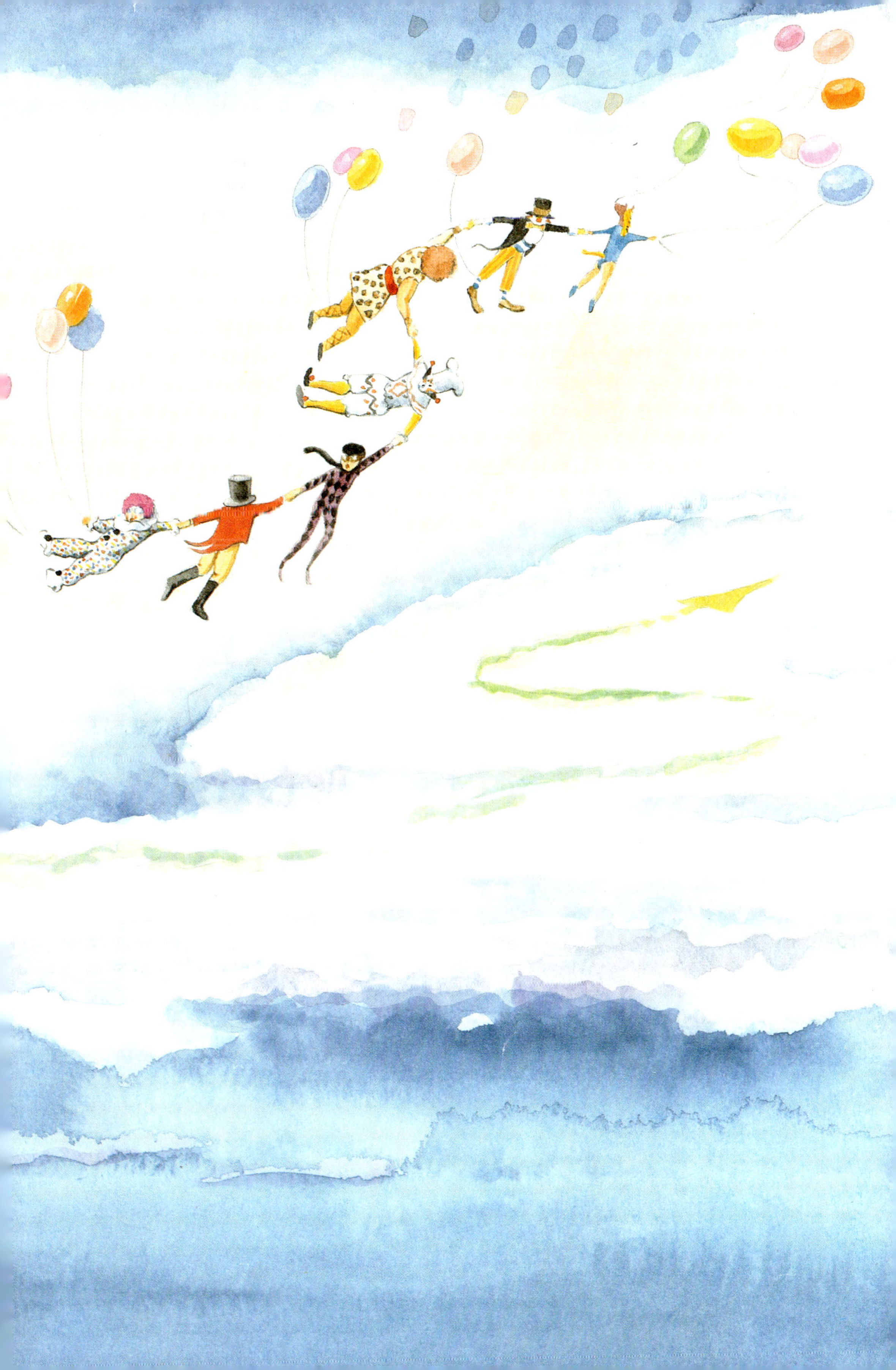

You can discover the day on which you, your relatives and friends, were born by visiting your local library and finding the Easy Reference Calendar in *Whitaker's Almanack*.

First published in Great Britain 1988
by Victor Gollancz Ltd
14 Henrietta Street, London WC2E 8QJ
© Michael Bragg 1988

British Library Cataloguing in Publication Data
Bragg, Michael
Monday's child.
I. Title
823'.914[J]   PZ7

ISBN 0-575-04097-1

Printed in Hong Kong by Imago Publishing Limited